PIPPBROOK BOOKS

First published in the UK in 1999 by Templar Publishing
This softback edition produced in 2013 by Pippbrook Books,
an imprint of The Templar Company Limited,
Deepdene Lodge, Deepdene Avenue, Dorking, Surrey, RH5 4AT, UK
www.templarco.co.uk

ISBN 978-1-84877-765-1

Designed by Hayley Bebb and Manhar Chauhan
Edited by Dugald Steer and Liza Miller

Printed in Singapore

# The
# BLACKBERRY
# MOUSE

WRITTEN BY MATTHEW GRIMSDALE    ILLUSTRATIONS BY TONY LINSELL

Mouse loved his little cottage in the country.
He loved it because it was warm and cosy,
and just the right size for a mouse.

Most of all he loved it because there was a BIG blackberry bush in the garden

and every year he had a bumper crop
of ripe, juicy blackberries.

One summer, Mouse's blackberries were even
bigger and juicier than usual. He began picking right
away and he was already hot and bothered when
Sparrow came by.

"What nice blackberries. May I have some?"
chirped Sparrow.
"They're all mine," said Mouse. "Go away!"
"No need to be rude," said the little bird,
and she flew away.

Mouse's paws were beginning to ache from
all the hard work when he caught sight of Squirrel.
"Can I have some of those juicy blackberries?"
Squirrel asked.
"If I give you some there will be less for me!"
Mouse replied. So Squirrel went away empty-handed.

Mouse had stopped to have a rest when Rabbit
came hopping through the grass.

"Those blackberries look delicious," she said.

"They are," said Mouse. "And I am going to eat every last one."

"Then you will most certainly be ill," said Rabbit,
and off she went.

The sun was hot and Mouse was getting very tired.
Soon he nodded off to sleep.
He didn't realise that someone had been watching him.

# It was Mr Fox...

When he saw that Mouse was asleep, he sneaked over
Mouse's gate and crept closer and closer until
he could pick up Mouse's basket.

He was just creeping away when—
SNAP!
He trod on a twig.

Mouse woke up with a start.
"Hey! Those are my blackberries!" he squeaked.
"You're far too small to stop me taking them,"
laughed Mr Fox. "They will make a fine tea for me."

Mouse was not surprised that
none of his woodland friends had warned him
Mr Fox was about. "After all," he thought,
"why should they help me when I would not
share my blackberries with them?"

Just then a strange thing happened.
An acorn landed on Mr Fox's head!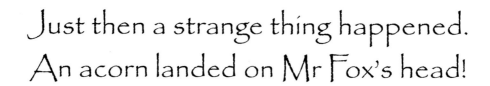

PLOP!

and another – PLOP!

And another, and another, and another.

PLOP! PLOP! PLOP!

Mr Fox dropped the blackberry basket and
ran away as fast as he could!

Mouse looked up to see where the acorns
had come from. And who do you think he saw
up in the old oak tree?

It was Squirrel and Sparrow and Rabbit.

"We couldn't let Mr Fox steal your
blackberries," said Squirrel. "Even if you
didn't want to share them," added Sparrow.

Mouse felt very ashamed.
Then he had an idea...

That afternoon Mouse invited everyone to a blackberry feast. He worked all day to get it ready.

There was blackberry juice to drink, blackberry jam, blackberry jelly, blackberry crumble, and lots and lots of little blackberry tarts.
The other animals said how delicious it all was.

"Perhaps," said Mouse, "blackberries are nicer if you share them, after all."